Tag Your Dreams

Poems of Play and Persistence

Jacqueline Jules   illustrated by **Iris Deppe**

Albert Whitman & Company
Chicago, Illinois

For Bill, who loved coaching and sports—JJ

For Cees, who lived to dance, teach, and inspire—ID

Library of Congress Cataloging-in-Publication data is on file with the publisher.

Text copyright © 2020 by Jacqueline Jules
Illustrations copyright © 2020 by Albert Whitman & Company
Illustrations by Iris Deppe
First published in the United States of America in 2020 by Albert Whitman & Company
ISBN 978-0-8075-6726-5 (hardcover)
ISBN 978-0-8075-6727-2 (ebook)

Printed in China
10 9 8 7 6 5 4 3 2 1 T&N 24 23 22 21 20 19

Design by Aphelandra Messer

For more information about Albert Whitman & Company,
visit our website at www.albertwhitman.com.

INTRODUCTION

Activity energizes me. Whenever I am stuck in a writing project, I take a walk around my neighborhood and let the ideas flow. If my legs move, my mind does too. I've solved many a plot problem on my feet.

Athletes inspire me. When I see an Olympic skater get right back up after a fall, it bolsters my own courage to try again after disappointment. And I am awestruck by a batter striding up to the plate, ready to focus on the next pitch, not the last strike. Bowling, basketball, swimming, tennis, tag, and even a piñata game can teach us a great deal about ourselves.

The poems in *Tag Your Dreams: Poems of Play and Persistence* celebrate being active, reaching goals, and learning limits. The narrators in these poems are boys and girls of different ages. But they have one thing in common. They discover themselves and their strengths through playing. I hope you will too.

—Jacqueline Jules

TAG YOUR DREAMS

Play tag
with your dreams.
Chase them
till you're breathless.
Dreams
have strong legs,
but so do you.
Keep running,
with your arm out,
fingers reaching.
Don't let them get away.

FOLLOW THE SIDEWALK

The sky is as gray
as a herd of elephants
gathering to stampede.

Thunder could be coming
this afternoon or evening.

But this moment offers
an early morning breeze
to kiss my cheek.

The pavement is still dry.

I'll take a chance
and follow the sidewalk
as far as it goes.

Hear my heart pound
in rhythm with my feet.

FOUR SQUARE RECESS

A big square on the playground
with four squares inside—
red, yellow, blue, green.

Faye gets there first. Then Cyrus,
then Sam. All of us breathless.
I take the last square.

Wait for the ball
to bounce just once
before I send it to Sam,
who smacks it to Faye,
who hurls it to Cyrus,
who hits the line.

He's out, and I shift a square
for Ella to enter the game.

I pass to the left, to the right,
across, again. Then I miss
and step off the court till
my next turn.

Round and round. Faster and faster.
Sometimes I'm on. Sometimes I'm out.

Who cares as long as
the game keeps moving,
and I still have the chance
to jump back in.

CLAPPING HANDS

Blanca sits on a blue bench,
brown eyes watching.

I'm close by, in my own seat
on wheels.

Does she have to be alone?
Do I?

Blanca sees me rolling
toward her. She doesn't look
away. Good sign.

"Do you know *Cho-co-la-te*?"

My legs can't run at recess,
but my hands can clap rhymes
my abuela taught me and reach
the new girl from Guatemala.

Choco, la, choco, te
Cho-co-la-te

Our hands fly
fast and strong
together.

PEDALING TO PIANO

Jenny Wilson fell off her bike,
banged her elbow,
ended up in a blue cast and sling.
She told everyone how
she heard her bone snap
when she hit concrete.

I thought about her
every Tuesday,
pedaling to piano.
It slowed me down,
as if I carried Jenny's cast
heavy on my shoulders.

Until the day
a squirrel
swerved in my path
and the brakes
I squeezed too hard
stopped me too fast.

Boom! Blood on my lip.
Bent wheel. Broken finger.

But no cast. No sling.
And an even bigger surprise
six weeks later
feeling no load on my shoulders,
pedaling to piano,
bike fixed, bone healed.

AT BAT

The pitcher throws the ball,
and decision splits the air.
Wait for the next one
or swing?
The right choice
mixed with luck and muscle
means the crowd will stand
and cheer.
Forget wrong decisions,
returning in silence
to sulk on the bench.
That was last time
and the time before.
I'll keep my eye
on the ball
and send fear
sailing
over the fence.

IN THE OUTFIELD

Glove raised, eyes
locked on the sky,
zipping back
till my toes
ache in my cleats.
So worried
the ball will drop
out of reach,
I almost forget
there's a fence
around the field
and if I don't
slow down soon
I will crash.

CARTWHEEL LESSON

I'm standing straight,
both arms in the air,
staring at Sue's finger
pointed at me.

She tells me it's easy
to be like her, do what she does.

Just put my palms on the ground
and face the sky with my feet.

"Hand, hand! Foot, foot!"
She claps and commands.

That's what it takes
to flip over
and see the world
from Sue's point of view.

I watch her hair touching the grass,
her limbs turning like bicycle spokes,
smoothly ending in a victory pose,
and think about my glasses dropping
on the ground. I feel my head ache.

Maybe Sue looks fine
walking on her hands,
but I feel better
balanced on my feet.

LAST PICK FOR KICKBALL

What?!?! Last?!?!

Lisa Watson's never liked me.
But I thought Abby did.

Good thing this game
gives me a chance
to kick the ball HARD.

Straight to the outfield,
where my anger shoots
over Abby's head
across the grass.

Now she's chasing
a red rubber ball
while I circle the bases
right past Lisa Watson's
bulging eyes, surprised
to see me score the way
I knew I could.

MERMAID MANATEE

You called me a name
this morning in the hall
on the way to math.
Come to the pool this afternoon.
You'll see the cow I really am—
sea cow, manatee—
graceful gray mammal
often mistaken for mermaid.

I twirl and glide,
long hair swirling around me,
skin glowing in the water.
It doesn't matter
that I am large and slow.
I am majestic. Worth
hanging over the rail to watch.

COURTSIDE SONG

Our rackets
still in sleeves,
we wait on the bench
beneath the lights,
restless feet
tapping
with the thump
of a yellow ball
on a hard green court.

The sound *pops* in dark air
while two girls in white shorts
and swinging ponytails
lunge and grunt for match point.

Their sneakers *squeak*
with the insects in the night,
promising our turn to play
if we'll only sit and sing
a patient tune.

STRINGS

Without a string,
a kite blows away
into the clouds,
having no one
who cares
how far it flies.

Without a string,
a mom can't hold a kite
while her daughter
runs across the field,
launching it into the wind.

Sure, a string gets tangled
sometimes. So twisted up,
it takes days to unravel.

And sometimes, a kite
wishes to be cut free,
to fly wherever it wants.

But without a string,
a kite is alone in the sky
with no one on the ground
watching and cheering.

KICK SCOOTERS

I brought my scooter
on my first visit to Dad's
new place on West 96th.

We left his third-floor walk-up
and spent the day at Central Park.

He was jealous of my bright green ride,
how I could just kick and zip ahead.

"Is it hard," he asked, "to balance
on two small wheels?"

"Not with the handle helping."

One question after another.
Dad trying to get me to talk.

It's not easy to have things
in common
every other weekend.

Unless you have a Dad like mine
who surprised me next time
by cruising through the park,
side by side, on matching scooters.

THE RIVER TRAIL

I was five the first time
Pops and Nana took me hiking.
We played "I spy" to find
a squirrel, a spider, a bird, a berry.
Stopped every half mile
for snacks and drinks.

The River Trail is still my favorite,
close to the red ranch house
where Nana and Pops lace their boots
and pack water, eager for adventure.

Traveling down a soft dirt path
we gaze at gray boulders dressed up in moss
and sycamore trees wrapped in mottled bark.

The trail rises, and we tread single file,
leaves rustling beneath our feet,
as a red-tailed hawk soars in a silent sky.

Resting at the top, we watch the water
rushing over rocks in foamy white swirls
and savor the green gracing this world
I learned to love when I was five.

MINI GOLF GIGGLE

My little brother skips
with bright red ball
and silver putter, ready
to test his power
over long green carpets
with holes at the end.

Gripping the black rubber handle,
he swings too hard. His red ball
circles the cup, crashes,
and careens. He giggles—
head back, small body bubbling
like the fountains beside us.

My turn. I model finesse
with a solid, smooth stroke
and a sky-blue ball that stops short,
six inches from the hole.

I tap it again. Watch it
bounce off the rim,
plop into water. I GROWL.

My little brother giggles.

The sound gurgles
down green slopes,
windmills and waterfalls,
sand traps and stones.

UMBRELLA DANCE

My baby sister, Mimi,
doesn't sit by the window
watching water fog the pane.

She doesn't pout
over canceled plans
at the beach.

She grabs her frog umbrella
and her plastic rainbow coat.

When she opens the door,
her polka-dot boots
pound the patio
louder than the rain.

She twirls, tongue out
to drink the drops.

My baby sister doesn't care
if the boy next door sees
or if anyone is laughing,
as long as she can dance
with her frog umbrella.

PIÑATA

My friends give me a stick,
tie a red cloth over my eyes,
and spin me in circles, laughing.

I swing again and again
at that candy-filled treasure
dangling just above my head.

No luck. Too bad. ¡Qué pena!

I take off the blindfold
and get back in line,
certain that all I need
is just one more swing,
and sweet surprises
will land at my feet.

#64 SOCCER TRYOUTS

I came early with new cleats,
shin guards, white socks.
My hair pulled off my face.
No earrings, no chains, no rings,
nothing to make the coach frown
as she judged with clipboard
and red pen, ready to mark
mistakes for #64.

Did she see
how many times
I touched the ball?
My ten shots? My speed?

I dribbled with both feet,
made a long pass,
even managed a Maradona.
All easier for me than the end
when I thanked the coach
and told her my name,
my eyes on hers, hoping
she'd remember #64
was Lainey Steele, not the shy girl
no one chose last season.

Coach smiled, marking
her clipboard with red pen.

I raced off the field,
arms raised, grinning.

All goals reached.

KNOCKING DOWN GHOSTS

I step onto the lane,
a shiny black ball
heavy in my hand.

Ten white pins in red bow ties
stand like ghosts
at the end of a glowing floor.

I hear them snicker
when my ball wobbles
into the gutter again.

For ten frames,
they rise with a cackle
and float back down
with a "BOO!"

Practice game over, I retie
my rented shoes, resolved.

This time, I'll knock down
those ghosts
and get a higher score.

TAE KWON DO

His leg spins
360 degrees,
and a bare foot
knocks me flat.

On the floor,
I breathe
till the knot
on my belt
rises.

Exhale.
Stand up.
Get ready to block
the next kick
when it comes.

REBOUNDING LUCK

Shot after shot
spins round
and round the rim,
slipping off
without a swish.

I want to stop and whine.
What's happening?

But my feet follow the ball,
back and forth, back and forth,
till my heart
is beating with the bounce.

Don't stop. Don't stop.

The words pulse from the floor,
daring me, daring me.

Don't stop. Don't stop.

Two seconds left,
down by one,
I grab that dare
and dunk it
through the hoop.

VOLLEYBALL

I serve by myself—
tossing high and jumping.

When my palm smacks the center,
the ball sails on my strength alone.

But it takes six on the court
to keep that tough white sphere
from dropping dead
on my side of the net.

Double hits are against the rules.
I can't touch that ball again
until a teammate has a turn.

Like it or not, this game
needs more than me to win.

ON THE PLAYGROUND

The long rope
swings in a circle,
slapping the ground
as everyone chants.

Uno, dos, tres...

Maria turns one end.
Sofia turns the other.
I'm in the middle,
then Rosa, then Carmen.

Cuatro, cinco, seis...

Our voices bounce and boom. Not
like Ms. Lynn's classroom, where
Spanish numbers do not sing.

Siete, ocho, nueve...

Heels lift.
Shoes thump.
We turn around.

Diez, once, doce...

On the playground
Spanish jumps
just as high as English.

FLAG FOOTBALL

Dad made me try it.
Said it was a way to learn the skills
without getting my brain busted.

Forget looking tough
like the players on TV.

No helmets or shoulder pads
to make me feel bigger than I am.

Just a jersey and a flag belt
fluttering off my skinny waist.

No tackling. No blocking.
No bodies slamming each other.

Not like Sunday TV.

But Dad only gave me one choice.

So I'm running, throwing, catching.
Learning offense, defense, teamwork.

Having fun with everybody else
in a game where nobody gets
knocked down.

RUNNING BACK

He's on the big screen again,
with padded shoulders,
and shiny tight pants.
The number on his jersey
identifies him clearly
for the cameras and the crowd,
as he clamps a strap under his chin,
without ever looking up.
I watch from my living room,
sometimes booing,
sometimes cheering,
but always wishing
I could put on a helmet
and run like that—
past all those guys
trying to knock me down—
not caring a bit
who's booing or who's cheering,
'cause I've got the ball in my hand.

THE HILL

Reaching the top,
my sled in my hands,
I'm bubbling inside.

Everything looks like
fluffy whipped cream
and smells as fresh
as peppermint.

The slope is long and wide
with a dip at the end.

I fly down, cool air
nipping my cheeks.

And trudge back up,
proud of the stripes
I left in the snow.

Again and again,
all afternoon.

My legs
never too tired
to climb the hill.

Though it seems
longer and longer
each time.

It's still a good trade
for the tingling thrill
of speeding
all the way down.

NOT TOO SMALL FOR A SNOWMAN

Since the day we moved to this block,
Mama's griped about our yard:
"No bigger than a card table!
Too small to play."

Until this morning
when we got out early,
before anyone shoveled,
to start at the corner,
where we had room to roll
three snowballs the size
of my brother's boot.

Down the sidewalk,
bigger and bigger.

Before long we had a body
to dress in a hot pink scarf
and floppy purple hat.

It was my sister's idea to add
sunglasses and a red licorice smile
after button eyes and a carrot nose.

Mama came out with hot chocolate
and new thoughts on our life in the city.

GRACELESS GIRL SKIS DOWN SLOPE

Slicing snow
on long narrow feet,
like a seaplane
spraying waves,
I sail down the slope,
leaving behind
the graceless girl
who couldn't play kickball
without a skinned knee.
At the top of the hill, she stares
openmouthed, beside Mr. Fine,
who gave me a C in phys ed.
They never saw me on snow,
swishing past trees,
my old self
spinning off
in a fine
white
powder.

OLYMPIC SKATER

Did you see
how he rose
after that fall?
In one sweeping
circular motion
as if the question
of getting up
never existed at all.
Now, with arms arched
toward the sky,
he soars with the music
to a second crescendo.
Spinning airborne,
he smiles,
as a medal whirls back
within reach.

FRESH ICE

We lost last time
and the time before.
That has nothing
to do with tonight.

Tonight,
home ice has a whole new surface,
shiny and smooth as a new skate blade.

Zamboni has shaved the old layer off
and left a magic mirror, reflecting
a scoreboard with zero under *Guest*.

All the fans settling
in stadium seats beside me
simmer with shared excitement.

We're ready to throw caps
and honor a hat trick—

three goals in a game—
from our star player.

Anything's possible
before the puck drops.

HOCKEY PUCK

Skaters with sticks
charge across the ice,
chasing
a round black disk—
slapping it back and forth
at 100 miles an hour.

I feel its pain,
struck over and over,
pushed forward and back,
blocked from its goal.

Everyone wants to control it.

But the puck is smart. Won't stay
in the curve of one stick
for too long. Circles the net.
Breaks free. Flies out of reach.

Shows guts.

ACKNOWLEDGMENTS

The author gratefully acknowledges the publications where the following poems first appeared, some in different versions.

Christian Science Monitor: "Graceless Girl Skis Down Slope"

Cricket Magazine: "At Bat," "Fresh Ice," "Olympic Skater"

The Poetry Friday Anthology, Pomelo Books: "Follow the Sidewalk," (previously "Racing the Clouds"), "Running Back"

YARN Young Adult Review Network: "In the Outfield" (previously "Watching the Wall"), "Hockey Puck," "Mermaid Manatee" (previously "Watch Me in Water"), "Piñata," "Rebounding Luck," "Tag Your Dreams," "Volleyball"

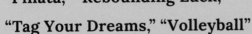